tiny Bible Tales

by W. C. Bauers

illustrated by Marta Costa

GROSSET & DUNLAP
An Imprint of Penguin Random House LLC, New York

Penguin supports copyright. Copyright fuels creativity, encourages diverse voices, promotes free speech, and creates a vibrant culture. Thank you for buying an authorized edition of this book and for complying with copyright laws by not reproducing, scanning, or distributing any part of it in any form without permission. You are supporting writers and allowing Penguin to continue to publish books for every reader.

Text copyright © 2018 by William Bauers. Illustrations copyright © 2018 by Penguin Random House LLC. All rights reserved. The stories in this book were originally published individually as board books in 2018 by Grosset & Dunlap. This bind-up edition published in 2019 by Grosset & Dunlap, an imprint of Penguin Random House LLC, New York. GROSSET & DUNLAP is a trademark of Penguin Random House LLC. Manufactured in China.

Visit us online at www.penguinrandomhouse.com.

The Library of Congress has cataloged the board book editions under the following Control Numbers:
Daniel in the Lions' Den: 2018285811, *David and the Lost Lamb*: 2018286323,
Jonah and the Whale: 2018286326, *Miriam and Pharaoh's Daughter*: 2018288157.

ISBN 9780593096215   10 9 8 7 6 5 4 3 2 1

David
and the Lost Lamb

Little David, shepherd boy,
brings his father so much joy.

Faithful in his daily task,
counting sheep from first to last.

Black, white, spotted, baa and bleat.
David loves the little sheep.

Little lamb goes off alone,
over hill and over stone.

In a valley, out of sight,
hungry lion wants a bite.

Mighty David blocks its way.
Swinging, roaring, saves the day.

Back in time for nighttime prayer,
keeps them safe from every care.

Little Jonah hears God say,
"Help the people to obey."

To the city, quickly go.
Stubborn Jonah answers, "No."

Tossed upon a stormy sea.
Sailors frightened as can be.

Overboard, into the waves.
Great whale opens, swallows, saves.

Three days in the deep and dark.
Change of ways, and change of heart.

Sweet forgiveness, answered prayer,
Jonah's spit into the air.

Back on dry ground, jumps with joy,
heads to town a faithful boy.

Miriam
and Pharaoh's Daughter

Little Miriam, quick to rise,
cradles brother, soothes his cries.

Trouble's coming, time to hide.
Baby takes a basket ride.

Down the bank, into the reeds.
Flowing river picks up speed.

Baby brother starts to cry.
Miriam sings a lullaby.

Pharaoh's daughter comes to bathe.
Drawn from water, baby's saved.

Loves the baby as her own,
knows that Moses needs a home.

Safe and sound, away from harm,
rocked to sleep in sister's arms.

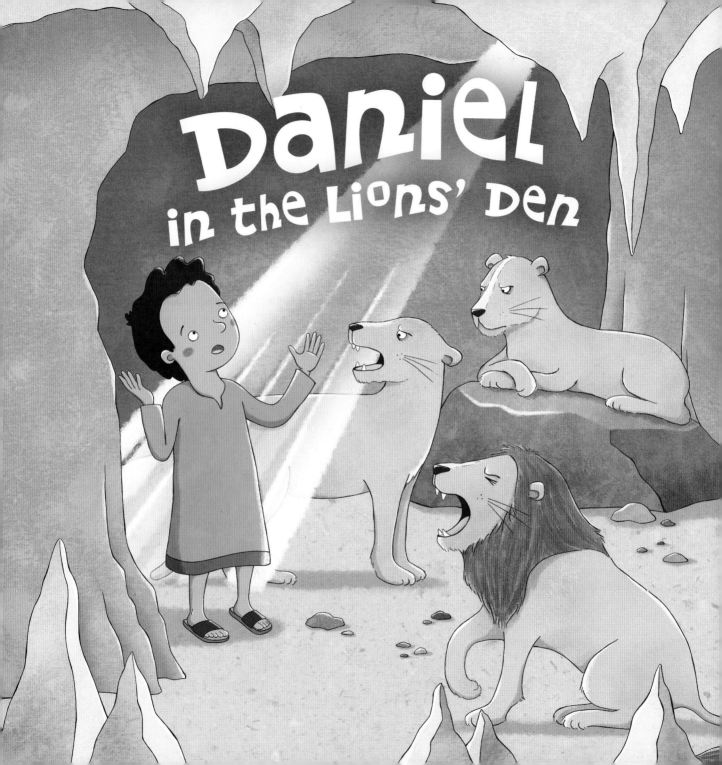

Little Daniel serves the king,
wise and good in everything.

Offers thanks in his own way.
Kneels in prayer three times a day.

When the king tells him to stop,
Daniel knows that he cannot.

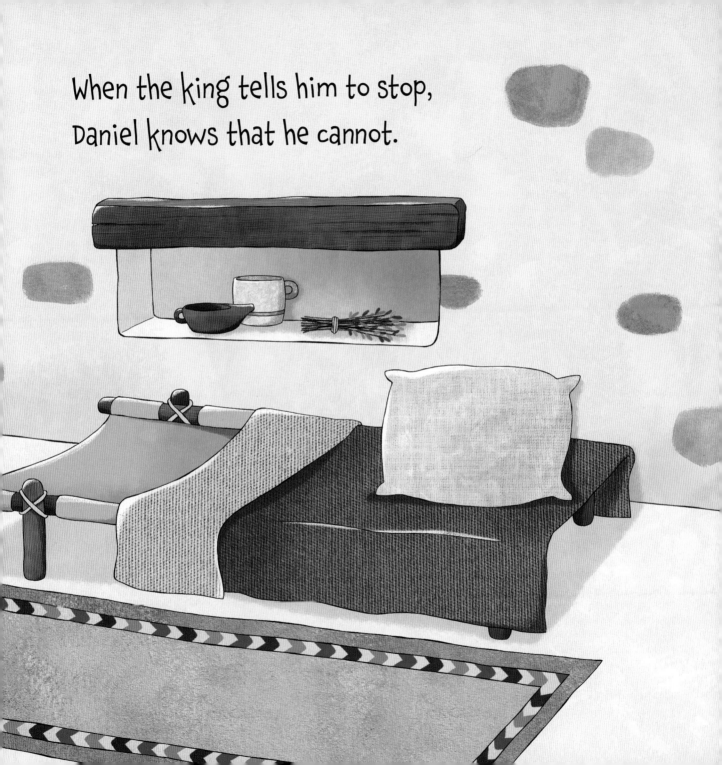

Thrown into the lions' den.
Great big stone to lock him in.

Hungry lions, scary sight.
Angel shuts their mouths up tight.

In the darkness until dawn.
Standing, stretching, morning yawn.

King is sorry, new decree.
Daniel's God has set him free.